Martin Waddell's classic and entirely original fable about justice made its first appearance on the inaugural list of then-new publisher Candlewick Press in 1992. With illustrations by multi-award-winning illustrator Helen Oxenbury, it didn't take long for the book to become a favorite with staff, booksellers, reviewers, librarians, and, of course, young readers, for whom fairness is all-important.

Twenty-five years after its first U.S. publication, the book and its enthusiastic reception remains a beloved and enduring piece of Candlewick history. More significantly, it continues to serve as a standard-bearer for what makes a perfect read-aloud picture book.

If you missed it the first time, here's your chance to take this modern classic to heart. And when you get to the part in the story when the lazy old farmer calls, "How goes the work?" *join in with the duck and answer,* "Quack!"

For Anna
M. W.

For Sebastian, David & C.P.
H. O.

Text copyright © 1991 by Martin Waddell
Illustrations copyright © 1991 by Helen Oxenbury

This U.S. edition 2017

The Library of Congress has cataloged the original hardcover edition as follows:

Waddell, Martin.
Farmer duck / Martin Waddell, Helen Oxenbury.
Summary: When a kind and hardworking duck nearly collapses from
overwork, while taking care of a farm because the owner is too lazy to do
so, the rest of the animals get together and chase the farmer out of town.
ISBN 978-1-56402-009-3 (original hardcover)
[1. Domestic animals—Fiction. 2. Farm life—Fiction.]
I. Oxenbury, Helen, ill. II. Title.
PZ7.W1137Far 1992
[E]—dc21   91-71855

ISBN 978-0-7636-8918-6 (twenty-fifth anniversary hardcover edition)
ISBN 978-0-7636-9561-3 (twenty-fifth anniversary paperback edition)

APS 21 20 19 18 17 16
10 9 8 7 6 5 4 3 2 1

Printed in Humen, Dongguan, China

This book was typeset in Veronan Light Educational.
The illustrations were done in watercolor.

Candlewick Press
99 Dover Street
Somerville, Massachusetts 02144

visit us at www.candlewick.com

FARMER DUCK

written by
MARTIN WADDELL

illustrated by
HELEN OXENBURY

CANDLEWICK PRESS

There once was a duck
who had the bad luck to live
with a lazy old farmer.
The duck did the work.
The farmer stayed
all day in bed.

The duck fetched the cow from the field.

"How goes the work?" called the farmer.

The duck answered,

"Quack!"

The duck brought the sheep from the hill.

"How goes the work?" called the farmer.

The duck answered,

"Quack!"

The duck put the hens in their house.

"How goes the work?"

called the farmer.

The duck answered,

"Quack!"

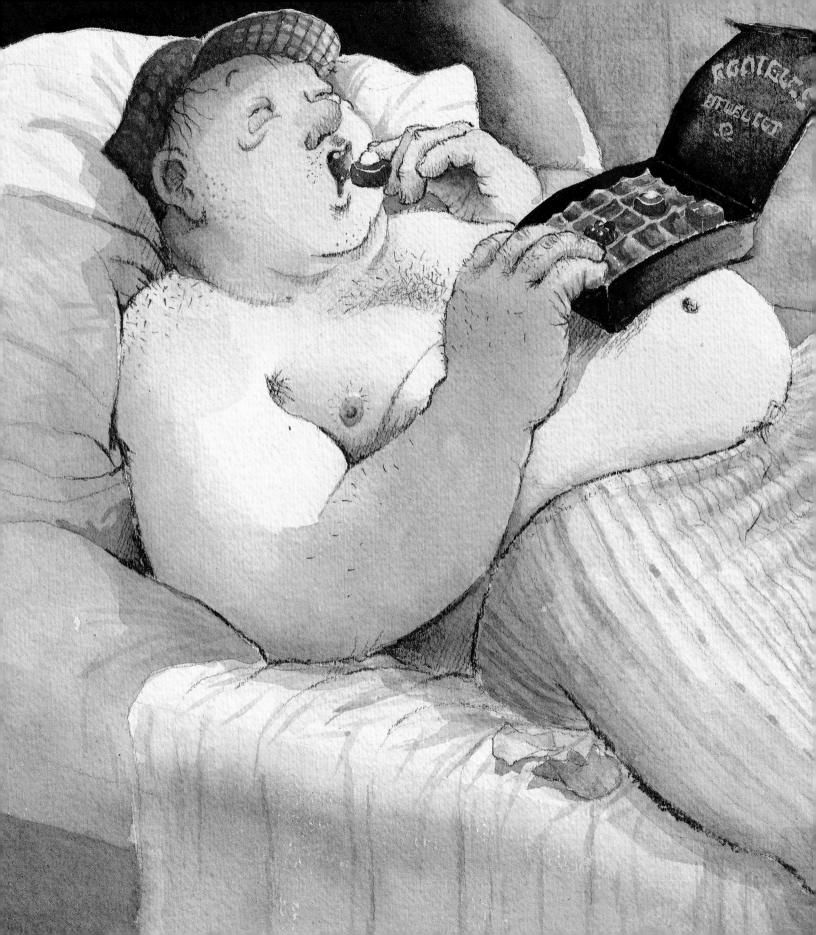

The farmer got fat through staying in bed,
and the poor duck got fed up
with working all day.

"How goes the work?"

"Quack!"

"How goes the work?"

"Quack!"

"How goes the work?"

"Quack!"

"How goes the work?"

"Quack!"

"How goes the work?"

"Quack!"

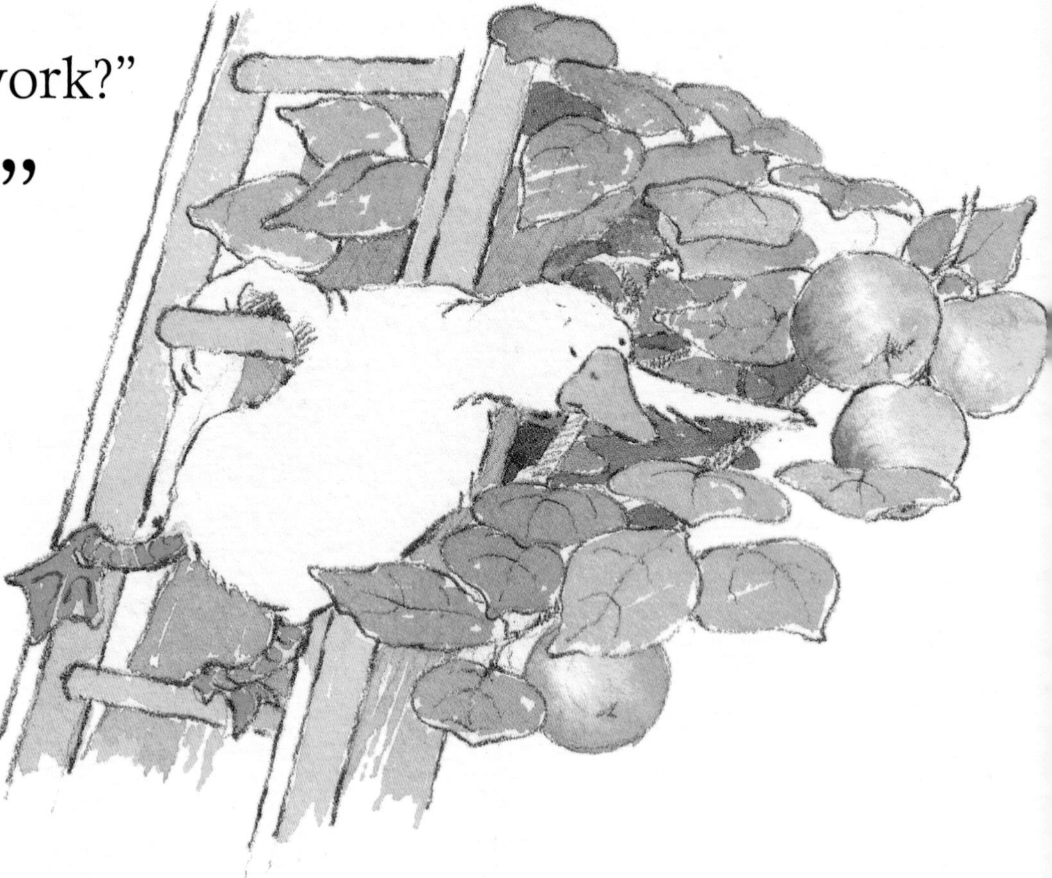

"How goes the work?"

"Quack!"

Soon, the poor duck grew
sleepy and weepy
and tired.

The hens and the cow and the
sheep got very upset.
They loved the duck.
So they held a meeting under
the moon, and they made
a plan for the morning.

"Moo!"

said the cow.

"Baa!"

said the sheep.

"Cluck!"

said the hens.

And *that* was the plan!

It was just before dawn and the farmyard was still.

Through the back door and into the house

crept the cow and the sheep

and the hens.

They stole
down the hall.
They creaked
up the stairs.

They squeezed under the bed of
the farmer and wriggled about.
The bed started to rock
and the farmer woke up,
and he called,
"How goes the work?"
and . . .

"Moo!"

"Baa!"

"Cluck!"

They lifted his bed
and he started to shout,
and they banged and they bounced
the old farmer about and about and about,
right out of the bed . . .

and he fled with the cow and the sheep and the hens

mooing and baaing and clucking around him.

Down the lane . . .

"Moo!"

through the fields . . .

"Baa!"

over the hill . . .

"Cluck!"

and he never came back.

The duck awoke and
waddled wearily into the
yard expecting to hear,
"How goes the work?"
But nobody spoke!

Then the cow and the sheep
and the hens came back.

"Quack?" asked the duck.

"Moo!" said the cow.

"Baa!" said the sheep.

"Cluck!" said the hens.

Which told the duck
the whole
story.

Then mooing and baaing
and clucking and quacking,
they all set to work
on their farm.